Robert the Bruce

by L DU GARDE PEACH OBE MA PhD DLitt
with illustrations by JOHN KENNEY

Ladybird Books Ltd Loughborough

ROBERT THE BRUCE

Although Robert Bruce was a great Scottish hero and patriot, much of his boyhood was spent in England. He was born in Scotland in 1274, but his father, who was also named Robert Bruce, had estates both in Scotland and in England, and his grandfather had married the daughter of the Earl of Gloucester.

The Robert Bruce whose story is told in this book, was the eighth to bear the same name. It was not, to begin with, a Scottish name at all. The first member of the Bruce family came over to England with William the Conqueror in 1066, and his name was Robert de Bruis. Bruis was the name of his castle near Cherbourg in France, and his name was changed to Bruce when he was granted estates in Yorkshire.

Young Robert Bruce grew up at the court of King Edward I of England. It was not a gay court, because King Edward was a famous soldier and law-giver, often away at the wars. It is probable that the young Robert Bruce rode out with the King, hunting and hawking.

It is certain that he grew up to be strong and fearless. He had need to be both in the years that followed.

At that time there was a King of Scotland as well as a King of England, and when in the year 1286, the King of Scotland died, there were two men who claimed the throne. They were Robert Bruce, grandfather of young Robert, and a man called John Balliol. Both were descended from King David of Scotland, who had reigned more than a hundred years before.

The Scots asked Edward of England to decide which should be King. A great gathering was held at Berwick, at which Edward gave the decision in favour of Balliol. Young Robert Bruce was eighteen years old at the time, and it is probable that he was at the conference with his grandfather.

When Edward awarded the Scottish crown to Balliol, he accepted it at first, but was soon raising an army to fight Edward. In order to get Bruce's family out of the way, Balliol gave all their Scottish estates to his nephew, John Comyn.

Naturally Robert Bruce fought on the side of Edward, and Balliol was beaten. Later another Scottish rebellion flared up, led by a patriot named Wallace. Bruce joined it, hoping it would succeed and that he himself would become King of Scotland.

Balliol was a prisoner in England, and Robert Bruce agreed to join John Comyn in ruling Scotland in his name. By doing this he secretly hoped to come a step nearer to becoming King of Scotland.

Although Bruce fought very successfully against the English, raiding the border counties and capturing many castles, his success only lasted a short while. Edward, returning from wars in France, again invaded Scotland, and the Scots were again defeated.

Bruce saw his hopes of becoming King of Scotland fading. He made peace with Edward and returned to the English court, but he was still secretly plotting with the Scots, hoping to start another war of independence.

Robert Bruce was now twenty-eight years old, tall, very strong and handsome, and popular with everybody at the English court. In the evenings the courtiers in their gaily coloured clothes would sit around the fire in the great hall of the palace, listening to a minstrel or story-teller. There would be very little comfort. Many of the lords and ladies would sit on stools or benches, but there were carpets brought from Spain, and there might be glass in the windows.

King Edward was warned that Bruce was secretly in communication with John Comyn, and there are strong reasons for believing that it was Comyn who betrayed Bruce. He probably hoped that Edward would have Bruce executed or at least imprisoned. This would have removed Comyn's only rival to the Scottish throne.

Edward was very angry, and there is no doubt that he would have had Bruce shut up in the Tower of London, or even put to death for treason. Bruce was warned by a friend who sent him a pair of spurs and some money. He understood that this meant he must escape immediately to Scotland.

He knew that Edward would send soldiers galloping after him, so he thought of a cunning way to put them off the trail. Before leaving he went to the blacksmith and had the iron horseshoes on his horses hooves turned the wrong way round. He hoped that this would make those who followed him think that they were the tracks of someone going in the other direction.

Unfortunately for Bruce the blacksmith betrayed him to the King, and soon armed men were after him, determined to kill him, if they could not take him alive.

Bruce had a long enough start to enable him to get safely to Scotland by riding hard, night and day. His first thought when he crossed the border was to settle with Comyn.

Comyn did not know that Bruce had discovered his treachery. When Bruce sent a messenger asking him to come to a meeting, Comyn thought that Bruce had decided to help him in again organizing revolt against the English.

They met in a church at Dumfries, and immediately Bruce accused Comyn of betraying him to the English King. Comyn, terrified of Bruce's anger, denied it, but the proof was too strong. Drawing his dagger, Bruce stabbed Comyn to death. As Balliol had fled to France seven years before, Bruce was now the only claimant with any real title to the Scottish throne.

They were rough, lawless times in Scotland, and human life was cheap. Comyn had deserved to die for his treachery towards Bruce. Most Scots, except the friends and relations of Comyn, approved of his death. They knew that with Robert Bruce as their leader, they had a better chance of winning the freedom and independence for Scotland which they all desired.

Bruce gathered his friends round him and rode with all speed to Scone. War with England was now certain, and Bruce intended to achieve his ambition of becoming King, and by doing so to rally all Scots to the defence of their country.

Already many of the Scottish nobles and bishops had joined him. His four brothers, Edward, Nigel, Thomas, and Alexander were of course on his side, as well as a young Scot, James Douglas, who was soon to become one of his most famous fighters.

Robert Bruce was crowned at Scone, the place where all Scottish kings were crowned, just as English kings are always crowned in Westminster Abbey.

The coronation ceremony had to be arranged in a hurry, and many of the ancient coronation robes were missing. It is recorded that even the crown was not to be found, and a plain gold band was used instead. More serious in the eyes of superstitious Scots, was the absence of the ancient Stone of Destiny, on which Scottish kings were crowned. It had been taken by Edward after the battle of Dunbar, and is still where he placed it, as part of the Coronation Throne in Westminster Abbey.

King Edward, now an old man, was very angry when he heard that Bruce had been crowned. He had believed that all Scottish resistance had been broken by the defeat of Wallace at Falkirk, and his subsequent execution. The defiance of Bruce, now Robert I of Scotland, meant that Edward would have to conquer the country all over again.

A great army was hastily gathered together, and the King vowed that he would never sleep two nights in the same place until he had conquered Scotland once and for all.

The story is told that when Edward made his vow he placed his hand on a golden net containing two swans. In those days when anyone made a vow or a promise it was usual to make it over some holy relic, or something which was supposed to make the promise more binding. Swans were believed to represent constancy and truth.

A proclamation was issued that all Scots who took up arms against England were to be beheaded, and the English estates in Durham and Middlesex which belonged to Bruce were confiscated. At the same time the Pope excommunicated Bruce for what he called the murder of Comyn in the church at Dumfries.

Bruce gathered a small army and retreated northwards, burning the crops and destroying everything which could be useful to the King's army, which was commanded by the Earl of Pembroke.

When Bruce reached Perth he decided to stand and fight, hoping that the English would be both weary and hungry.

It is not easy for us to understand what battles were like in those days, and things happened which would to-day be impossible. When the English reached Perth they halted, and the two armies were face to face. Bruce immediately sent a messenger challenging Pembroke to come into the open space between the armies and fight it out, man to man.

There was nothing surprising in this, nor was Bruce surprised when Pembroke replied politely that he was tired and would prefer to wait until the morning. The Scots settled down for the night, fully expecting to watch a duel between their two leaders in the morning. After that had been decided, one way or the other, there might or might not be a battle. But Pembroke had no intention of meeting Bruce in personal combat. Suddenly, in the night, he treacherously attacked the sleeping Scots, and they were overwhelmed and scattered.

Bruce escaped with only two or three hundred men, the remnant of his army. They retreated into the wild hills to the north of Perth, where for the time they were safe.

Edward was determined to stamp out rebellion in Scotland once and for all. Prisoners were executed and anyone suspected of helping Bruce was hanged. Even the women were not spared. Edward ordered that Bruce's wife and sisters were to be regarded as outlaws, which meant that anyone could rob or even kill them without suffering any penalty.

They at once fled to join Bruce in the mountains. Then, as to-day, a large part of Scotland consisted of rugged hills and glens, wild and desolate, without roads or houses or any kind of shelter.

It was a hard, rough life, hunting the deer and fishing for food, or gathering the whinberries which grew wild amongst the heather. The fugitives had continually to retreat further into the hills to avoid the search parties sent out by Pembroke to catch them. They lived in caves or in rough shelters made of branches and the skins of deer. Such a life could be not unpleasant in fine summer weather, but when autumn came it was cold and wet.

Homeless wandering in the Scottish highlands in winter was too great a hardship for Bruce's wife and sisters. So they went to a northern castle which belonged to Bruce's brother Nigel. Here Bruce hoped that they would be safe.

Unfortunately the castle was captured by the King's army, and Bruce's wife, sisters, and other ladies were taken prisoners. Edward had no mercy, even on helpless women; he ordered them to be confined in wooden cages, some in Berwick and some in the Tower of London.

Meanwhile Bruce was marching on foot to the west of Scotland. Not only was he obliged to avoid parties of English soldiers, but many of the Scots were also his enemies. These were the relatives and followers of John Comyn, and they were determined to avenge the killing of their kinsman.

On their way Bruce and his men came to Loch Lomond. To march round it would have taken them into the country of their enemies, so they were obliged to cross it. All they could find was a small boat which would only take two at a time. Whilst they awaited their turn for the boat, Bruce told them stories of knightly adventures to keep up their spirits.

Everyone knows the story of Bruce and the spider. When a man becomes a national hero all sorts of stories are told about him, some true, some not so true. What is true is that for Bruce everything looked hopeless.

He was in hiding on one of the islands off the west coast, and he knew that most of Scotland was in the hands of people, Scottish and English, who were determined to kill him if they found him.

Added to this, many of his most trusted followers had been captured and executed, and news had been brought to him of the way in which Edward had imprisoned his wife and his sisters.

Bruce must have spent long hours wondering and planning what to do. At such a time, when people are thinking deeply, their eyes often seem to be staring at nothing. Then some movement catches their attention. We must also remember that in those days people were very superstitious. The movement of a spider trying to spin its web and failing time after time, may have caught Bruce's eye, and he may well have said to himself, if the spider succeeds, I shall succeed. The spider succeeded, and Bruce took heart again.

It may have been watching a spider which encouraged Bruce to continue the fight to free Scotland. In any case, he now determined that he would return to the mainland and try again. On the way back, on the Isle of Arran, he found James Douglas and some of his followers.

James Douglas, who was called Black Douglas because of his black hair, was one of the most gallant of the young Scottish nobles who fought with Bruce against the English. It was now decided that he and another of Bruce's followers should cross the narrow water to Scotland and find out whether the men of that part of the country were ready to rise against Edward.

It was arranged that if they were, a bonfire should be lit on a hill. As soon as he saw it, Bruce and the men with him were to cross to the mainland.

Night after night they waited, watching for the fire on the hilltop. Then suddenly one blazed up, and they took to the boats. But when they landed they were told that it was the heather on the hillside which was burning. The whole of that part of the country was swarming with English soldiers.

Bruce gathered what few men he could and attacked and defeated a small English garrison in a village. His presence in the country now became known, and when he retired again into the wild hills of Galloway, the English completely surrounded him.

The only thing for Bruce to do was to break out through the encircling forces. He divided his little army into three, so that the English would not know which to follow. But the English had a bloodhound which had once belonged to Bruce, and it faithfully followed its master's trail. It was only by wading along a stream, and so destroying the scent, that Bruce escaped.

More and more men were joining Bruce, and the Earl of Pembroke learnt that the Scots were gathered in a glen called Glentrool. He advanced to the attack, but Bruce, warned that they were coming, had stationed his men in hiding on the hillside.

The English were straggling along the narrow road between the steep hillside and the loch when suddenly a shower of arrows struck them. Then came a charge of Bruce's men down the steep slopes. The English were unable to form up to defend themselves, and they were cut to pieces.

By quickly moving from place to place amongst the hills, Bruce was able to overcome, one after another, the groups of men who were searching for him. But these were small successes and the liberation of Scotland seemed as far away as ever.

Then Edward I, who was with his main army at Carlisle, died. On his tomb in Westminster Abbey are the Latin words, *Scottorum Malleus*, which means the 'Hammer of the Scots'. He had certainly been like a hammer beating down Scottish freedom, but he had not beaten the Scots into submission.

Edward II was now King, but he was a very different man from his father. He had little interest in war with Scotland, and very soon he marched back to London, taking the army with him. In Scotland there were now only the few English garrisons holding castles up and down the country.

Robert Bruce was now able to turn on those of the Scots who had been fighting against him, not because they were friends of the English, but because they were followers or relatives of John Comyn. They were fighting for revenge. By swift campaigns Bruce beat them in the field and captured their strongholds.

Robert Bruce, now thirty-five years old, was at last able to consider himself King of Scotland in more than merely King in name. He was able to summon regular parliaments at St. Andrews, and to govern the country.

He did more. Edward II had marched away, but there had been no peace treaty. So Bruce sent Black Douglas south to carry the war into the northern counties of England.

On the way Douglas determined to recapture his own castle, which had been taken and garrisoned by the English. He had very few men with him, so he waited until a day when the English garrison left the castle to go to the church in the village. Douglas's men mingled with the English, who had no idea that there were any enemies within miles of them. At a given signal the Scots struck down the unsuspecting soldiers.

Douglas and his men then marched back to the castle. They had overcome the English so quickly that no alarm had been given, and they found the castle gate open and the cooks busy preparing dinner for the English garrison. But it was the Scots, not the English, who ate it.

Edinburgh castle was still held by the English. High up above the town on a great rock, it was heavily fortified, and no army of the time could ever have taken it by assault.

Fortune was on the side of Bruce. One of his commanders, the Earl of Morray, met a young Scotsman whose father had once been the Governor of Edinburgh castle. The Governor had been very strict. No-one had been allowed to leave the castle, but his son, whose name was Francis, had friends in Edinburgh whom he wished to visit from time to time. So he had found a way by which he could climb down the rock.

It was a dangerous and difficult climb, but Francis knew every crack and foothold. He was sure that he could lead a small party of men up to the castle wall without their presence being suspected by the sentries.

So one very dark night the Earl of Morray and a party of Scottish soldiers followed Francis to the foot of the great rock. Slowly and silently they climbed in the darkness. The sentries, suspecting nothing, were overpowered, and soon Edinburgh Castle was again in the hands of the Scots.

Most of the castles in Scotland were now held by Bruce. One of the strongest, Stirling Castle, still contained an English garrison. They could not get out because Bruce's men were closely beseiging it, but if Bruce marched away there would be another band of English soldiers free to raid the Scottish lowlands.

Then the Governor of Stirling Castle made a bargain with Bruce's brother Edward. He promised to surrender the castle if he were not relieved by Midsummer day.

It is difficult for us to-day to think of such a bargain between two deadly enemies, but such things were not uncommon in the middle ages.

Provisions were running short in Stirling Castle, and with a whole garrison to feed, the Governor knew that soon they would be starving. Bruce could, of course, have waited until they were starved into surrender, but there was a code of chivalry which often tempered the fierceness of the middle ages. Perhaps also Bruce wanted to finish the war once and for all. So he agreed and allowed the Governor to send a messenger to Edward II asking for an army to come and relieve the castle. Bruce gathered his forces for the expected battle.

Edward II was not as good a general as his father had been, but he realised that if Stirling Castle surrendered he would have lost Scotland. He sent messengers throughout England and to his domains in France, to summon the greatest army ever up to that time gathered on English soil.

There was in those days no regular army. The great nobles were allowed to hold their estates in return for military service, and each in accordance with his rank had to bring so many men to the King's army. A duke might bring many hundreds, all armed at his expense, but a simple knight was expected only to bring ten or twenty men.

Another thing which made it difficult to keep an army together was that the nobles and knights were obliged only to serve in it for so many days each year. When they had done so, they were free to go home, taking all their men with them.

The army which Edward II gathered to relieve Stirling Castle must have been a fine sight. All the nobles would be in armour and carrying gaily painted shields, with hundreds of silken banners fluttering above.

We do not know how many soldiers were in Edward's army, but it could not have been more than about twenty thousand, of whom some two thousand .were knights in full armour. We do know that the long train of supply waggons stretched for twenty miles.

Bruce had less than half this number of men, but Bruce was a better general than Edward. His men were fighting for their native land and with hatred in their hearts; Edward's men were invaders.

Bruce waited behind a little stream called Bannock burn, not far from Stirling Castle. When the English army arrived, one of those things happened which made battles in the middle ages so different from those of later years. An English knight, Henry de Bohun, rode out and challenged Bruce to single combat.

Bruce was unarmed, except for his battle-axe, and he was riding a small pony. De Bohun was fully armed on his great war horse. They met in full view of the two armies, the Englishman with his long lance aimed straight at Bruce. At the last moment Bruce swerved aside, and as de Bohun swept past, struck him to the ground with one blow of his battle-axe.

The battle of Bannockburn was fought on a lovely June day in the year 1314. It ended in a disastrous defeat for the English army.

The English knights were brave men and good fighters, but they had never been drilled to charge like a troop of cavalry. They rushed into a battle, each man for himself, caring little what happened to the others. Bruce had very few horsemen, but his foot-soldiers were strong and sturdy, and each was armed with a long pike. Bruce had trained them to remain together, with their pikes held pointed outwards all round, like the spines of a hedgehog.

Bruce had taken up a position on a low hill protected by the marshy bed of the Bannock burn, or stream. On the left the stream ran round the end of the hill, and on the right his position was protected by wooded country through which the English horsemen could not advance.

Early in the morning of June 24th, Bruce arranged his army in order of battle. In front were three bodies of pikemen, with another in reserve, whilst a squadron of 500 horsemen was held ready to charge at the right moment.

The armies were within a few hundred yards of one another, and the Scots knelt for a moment for a blessing by the Abbot of Inchaffray. Edward, seeing them on their knees, cried "Ha! They kneel for mercy!" He was wrong.

At once the English trumpets sounded for the attack, and Bruce's men rose to receive the charge of the English knights. Many fell on the Scottish spears, and soon the numbers of dead and wounded, and the wild plunging of riderless horses, prevented those in the second and third ranks from reaching the Scottish pikemen.

Hemmed in between the marshy ground and the stream, they could not open their ranks, and the long pikes of the Scots pressed the front ranks back on those behind.

A charge by Bruce's mounted men-at-arms dispersed the English archers, and the sudden appearance over the hill of a number of Scottish servants and camp followers, mistaken by the English for reinforcements, caused the great army raised by Edward for the conquest of Scotland, to break and flee. Edward himself galloped from the field pursued by Scottish horsemen, but managed to get clear away. He is said never to have slowed down until he reached Dunbar.

The English fled from the field of Bannock-burn leaving behind them booty said to have been worth five million pounds. What was more important for Bruce, they left a number of prisoners in the hands of the Scots. One of these, the Earl of Hereford, was exchanged for Bruce's wife and sisters.

Bruce was now truly master of Scotland and offered to make peace with England. Edward refused, and for thirteen years Bruce and Douglas carried the war into northern England. Time and time again the Scots raided Cumberland and Westmorland, and devastated the countryside as far south as York.

In Scotland people were enjoying a period of peace. The Scottish parliament was meeting, passing laws to regulate the affairs of the kingdom and its trade beyond the seas.

Edward II still refused to sign a peace treaty with Scotland, although the people who lived in the north of England were weary of the slaughter and desolation due to the ever recurring raids by the victorious Scots. Once more the English attempted to invade Scotland, but were every-where beaten back, until Edward II was deposed. With his young son on the throne, peace with Scotland was possible.

Bruce had always wished to live at peace with England, but only if England were prepared to recognise Scotland as a free country under its own King. He welcomed the peace conference at Northampton.

He had succeeded in his life's work. Scotland was free at last. What was more, the treaty recognised Bruce as "our dearest ally and friend, the magnificent prince, Lord Robert, illustrious King of Scotland". If Bruce had known, when he was a fugitive in the Western Isles, that a King of England was one day to address him in these words, he would not have required a spider to encourage him.

Scotland was to be "separate in all things from the kingdom of England, whole, free, and un-disturbed." It was to remain so for 275 years, until a Scottish King became King also of England.

The union of the two countries might have come about sooner. When peace was declared it was arranged that Bruce's son, David, should be married to Joanna, the six-year-old sister of Edward III. The marriage took place later at Berwick, but Bruce was not able to be present. He had been taken ill with a mysterious disease and the following year, in 1329, he died.

Much of Scotland remains to-day as Bruce knew it when, a homeless fugitive from the English, he took to the hills of the north. The bleak moors and the deep wooded glens are many of them as pathless and difficult to reach as they were in 1300.

In those days Scotland was a poor country, sparsely inhabited, and it would have seemed to most men an impossible task to raise an army capable of fighting the might of England. Even when the men had been mustered, they were as inferior to their enemies in weapons as they were in numbers.

They would look very unlike an army if we could see them to-day, but what they lacked in arms, they made up in fierce patriotism. Above all, they were commanded by Robert the Bruce.

Bruce was a great man, as well as a great patriot. He never gave up, even when everything was against him, and no man ever fought against greater odds, and won. He re-created the Scottish nation by his gift of leadership and great personal courage. When people remembered all that he had done, it was said of him that he never forgot his friends, and often forgave his enemies.

Showman
and his bear

Man
with sling
scaring birds

Hawking

A Castle

Oak Chest

A Tinker

Keys